A is for A L I E N ™

An ABC Book

Adapted by Charles Gould
Illustrated by Joey Chou
Based on the screenplay by Dan O'Bannon and Ronald Shusett

 A GOLDEN BOOK • NEW YORK

© 2024 20th Century Studios. Published in the United States by Golden Books, an imprint of Random House Children's Books, a division of Penguin Random House LLC, 1745 Broadway, New York, NY 10019, and in Canada by Penguin Random House Canada Limited, Toronto. Golden Books, A Golden Book, A Little Golden Book, the G colophon, and the distinctive gold spine are registered trademarks of Penguin Random House LLC.
rhcbooks.com
ISBN 978-0-7364-4484-2 (trade) — ISBN 978-0-7364-4485-9 (ebook)
Editor: Geof Smith I Designer: Xiomara Nieves I Copy Editor: Debra DeFord-Minerva
Managing Editor: Cindy Johnson I Production Manager: Mary Ellen Owens
Printed in the United States of America
10 9 8 7 6 5 4

A is for alien.

That's something you might meet in space.

B is for button.

Don't press it, or you could let the alien in!

C is for crew. They want to know where their visitor is.

Kane   Lambert   Parker   Ripley   Ash   Brett

Jones

D is for Dallas. He's the captain. He'll find it!

E is for egg. What could be inside this strange thing?

G is for growing. The alien is small, but it keeps getting bigger!

H is for "Help! Brett found the alien!"

I is for investigate. The crew searches the ship to find the creature.

J is for Jones—the ship's cat,
who pops up without warning.

K is for Kane. He doesn't feel well. His tummy is rumbling.

L is for Lambert. Now she's not sure she wants lunch.

M is for Mother.

She's the computer that runs the spaceship. Maybe she can help!

N is for *Nostromo*. That's the name of the big ship everyone's on.

O is for open. Time to unlock the air vent and look inside.

Who wants to go first?

P is for Parker. He's looking for supplies.

Q is for quiet.

Don't make a noise, or
the alien will hear you!

R is for Ripley. She's ready to take charge.

S is for secret. Ash, the science officer, knows one . . . or two.

T is for tracker. It shows that the alien is moving!

U is for "Uh-oh! It's coming this way!"

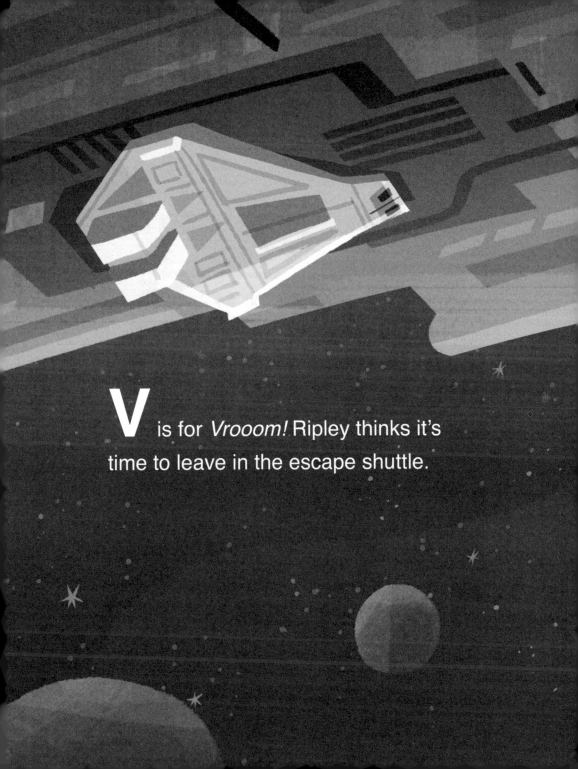

V is for *Vrooom!* Ripley thinks it's time to leave in the escape shuttle.

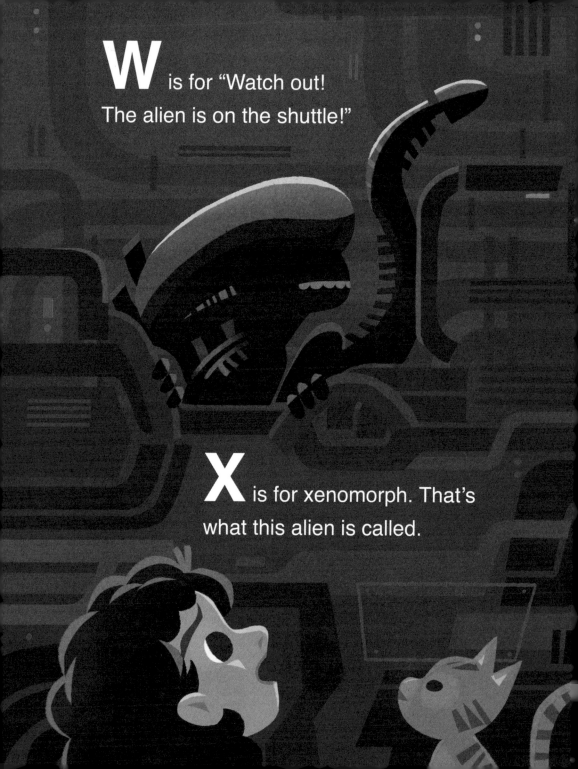

W is for "Watch out!
The alien is on the shuttle!"

X is for xenomorph. That's
what this alien is called.

Y is for "Yay! The alien is gone!"

Z is for *Zzzzz*. Sleep tight, Ripley.